The Book of Sounds

Mehdi Navid

Translated by
Tina Rahimi

the operating system print//document

The Book of Sounds

ISBN: 978-1-946031-42-6
Library of Congress Control Number: 978-1-946031-29-7

edited and designed by ELÆ [Lynne DeSilva-Johnson]
translation/editorial assistant: Ashkan Eslami Fard

The English text was set in Tox Typewriter Minion, Franchise, and OCR-A Standard. Farsi was set in N-Rooznameh and N-Ketab-Tookhali

The cover image is from artist Iman Raad. More at http://www.imanraad.com

Books from The Operating System are distributed to the trade by SPD/Small Press Distribution, with ePub and POD via Ingram, with production by Spencer Printing, in Honesdale, PA, in the USA.

Your donation makes our publications, platform and programs possible! We <3 You.
http://www.theoperatingsystem.org/subscribe-join/

the operating system
www.theoperatingsystem.org

The Book of Sounds

2018-19 OS System Operators

The operating system is a member of the **Radical Open Access Collective**, a community of scholar-led, not-for-profit presses, journals and other open access projects. Now consisting of 40 members, we promote a progressive vision for open publishing in the humanities and social sciences.

Learn more at: http://radicaloa.disruptivemedia.org.uk/about/

The Book of Sounds

Mehdi Navid

Translated by
Tina Rahimi

For Tahoora,
in the morning,
at noon,
in the evening

In this landscape, most people are fictitious. Any resemblance between them and any real person should be regretted by that real person.

Ebrahim Golestan

night

1

The novel starts on the stairs of a passenger bus, coming to contact with Anis' shoes out of the blue. We have to be really careful here, in describing the period of time elapsed, as the shoes come to contact with each stair. In each contact, the sounds around the bus become more vibrant and speed up, but the contact itself is dim and slow; it doesn't hurt the ear. But we stay right here. There is much noise in the air, and we focus on the brief conversations between the passengers and the crew; most of the conversations are around the destination, when the bus would leave, and the passengers' luggage. From the last stair, where Anis' shoes twirl on to get to her seat, to where Anis' hands take off her backpack in order to push it in the storage compartment above her head, we do not see anything; not even her eyes scanning others as they are scuttling through the narrow aisle between the seats. We see the comfort of her body spreading against the seat. Registering the light inside the bus is of utmost importance here. The sounds, too... less important, though. Then, all is soaked in white.

2

Anis' backpack glides on the bed, all the way to Anis' chin and then, her look. The sound of gliding may not matter in describing the setting, but we have to be careful about Anis' eyelids, opening and closing, specifically, the closing of the eyelids... Anis' not-seeings. At one with Anis' look, we see the small room and a bunk, Anis and the backpack now unzipped, and Anis' hand, as if eternally groping. Nothing comes out of the backpack, ever, Anis' eyes are closing, the lids become less, slower. Night.

3

Anis' eyes, on a cold, late afternoon, follow people and walls. She is supposed to go inside the publishing company. She, Anis, has edited a book.

Anis' hands, in the manager's office, do not have anything to do but to talk. We do not see the manager's mouth; we just hear that he is happy and pleased with Anis visiting. A conversation takes shape between them, about work. Anis' lips, during the conversation, are calmly restless to be somewhere else. The conversation, however short, has to be written in a manner that conveys dimness and slowness; the atmosphere is not cold at all, but the restlessness and anticipation have to be perfectly described. The door squeaking when Anis' feet exit.

(It seems that the location of the publishing company matters, particularly for the following scenes: the building is located in front of a big motor vehicle overpass. Under it, there are a few bookstores, and somehow, they have formed a bookstore block. The building itself is old and the publishing company is lodged on the second floor. The stairs, all the way up, are made of granite, still preserving their old identity. Yet, the door and the setting inside do not carry a trace of time. Everything is brand new: the paint on the walls, the desks and chairs, and even the blinds and windows. The only thing that stands out in this modern setting is the squeaking of the doors. But it seems that the noise doesn't bother anyone, or else, they would have them oiled; the hinges.)

4

Anis' wavering steps, when she enters the editing office, should convey to the reader that Anis has already worked here for a week before coming to the conclusion that her talent is being wasted here and that she cannot attend to her own concerns any longer. And that is why Anis has left the company after making excuses, announcing to the manager that her father wanted her to go back to Shiraz, and now that she has finished school, he doesn't want her to work at Tehran anymore. The manager has tried to calm Anis down and tell her to listen to her father, because her father has her best interests at heart. But we also know that Anis has been desperate for the money she has been making at this job in order to stay in Tehran and attend to her own business: writing. However,

Anis returns to Shiraz and accepts an editing job offered to her by the publishing company in order to keep bread on the table and to do what she likes.

After the wavering steps of Anis enters the office, Mr. Mozdarani gets up and smiling, asks her for a souvenir, without greeting her. Anis' hands touch the solid surface of the wooden desk she has worked at for a week, and then, Anis' bottom places itself on the chair behind the desk. And Anis' parched lips along with her hand, now lifted up from the surface of the desk, say that they have brought masqati, only for the manager. Mozdarani, as if offended, leaves the office and goes to the manager and picks up the masqati box; probably with the excuse of offering it to all the employees. And he does that, too. Then, he comes back to Anis, but he doesn't offer anything to her. Anis' eyes, shocked from Mozdarani' gesture in snatching the masqati box from the manager, stay at the bottom of the eye sockets, but Anis' lips are searching for somewhere else, so they bring up the search for a new editing job, so that they can get out of there, as soon as possible, in one piece.

Mozdarani has thick lips, but when he speaks, it is as if they are lazy and don't move that much, meaning that they are not seen. Only the lines on his face, and his eyes are gorged with blood . Anis' ears realize that he would not give the next available job to her, because he, Mozdarani, leaves everything to "later". Anis' eyes follow the sound of a crow, sitting right behind Mozdarani across the window, on a tree. Mozdarani, voice is loud, but Anis knows that her eyes should be content with the sound of the crow, and let the time pass.

We should also consider the fact that while narrating this scene, a young man enters: the one for whom Anis' lips are restless. It is better that Anis go to the kitchen when Mozdarani goes to get the masqati box from the manager, and quite accidentally, see the young man standing on the kitchen's balcony, smoking. In the solitude and silence of the kitchen, their lips curl around each others' neck and shoulders. Along with the rest of her face, Anis' cheeks, all of a sudden, as if remembering something, turn around, and from the editing office, Anis' hands bring the wine Anis had brought from Shiraz for the young man. Mozdarani is still offering masqati to the coworkers, but his ears see that Anis' happy hands take a silver bag to the kitchen, and then, emptied and free, they come back to the editing office, and afterwards, the young man comes out of the kitchen, with the same silver rustling.

5

Anis' eyes, when hand in the young man's hand, she steps down the stairs of the publishing company. Anis' shoulders gently brushing against the young man, turning around in the landing. Their steps, echoing the sound of happiness in the air; as if the shoes are galloping on the stairs.

The setting is as such that we know, when the feet of Anis and the young man cross the doorway of the building, they are about to go to the young man's apartment, so no hesitation is allowed in front of the doorway. From this point on, we do not see any longer, how Anis and the young man, now slowing down, walk down the street leading to the young man's place, and go shopping for their night; but it's not a bad idea to check out the noises of the street and to describe the many cabs steering around without any passengers, and for sure, when passing by the handicraft stores or the pastry shops or the supermarkets, the green or the yellow of their bodies, for a moment, as short as possible, have crashed into the clutched hands of Anis and young man, walking down the sidewalk. We should remember that in this momentary passage, we do not need the voice of the people on this street, not even the voice of the cab drivers ruthlessly competing for passengers.

We still do not see that Anis and the young man are done with shopping, and that the young man has taken a detour to show Anis the old houses back alleys, whose old beautiful architecture is very enticing. Anis has yielded to the temptation of the houses, but cheerfully, has mentioned Shiraz, and the young man has realized that showing these houses to her is like bringing sand to the beach. Then, both have laughed, and Anis' hand has looked at the young man's hand again, and has snatched it away in an instant.

6

The sound of a key turning in the door lock, and then, the sound of the guy's shoes, entering, followed by Anis' eyes, stopping to listen to the sound of the house, and then Anis' smile which colors the books on the guy's bookshelves. The guy, alone, has changed in the bedroom by now and has returned to Anis' look. Anis' feet have taken the path to the bedroom and have gone, then have returned, and without socks, have relaxed on the sofa, next to the guy.

From this point on, till the time Anis' hand suddenly remembers the wine, a conversation starts between them. This conversation entails a particular finesse, because it is both about literature and their lifestyle; as if two people have sat next to one another and decided to reveal everything to each other in the fraction of a second. But the complexity of this conversation also entails another type of finesse: it seems that they both know each other enough, as if this friendship has been there for years. The reader, of course, knows that this is not so, in fact, but it is the lived experiences they have in common, which have shuffled them together. One of the important factors to be considered in arranging the conversation is playing around with Anis' hands and the guy's sitting pose, and of course, a short but big hexagon table, and the sound of the books being taken out of the bookshelves mixing with the sound of eyelids. Here, we do not hear Anis' cell phone ringing a couple of times, not even the occasional TV sound the guy keeps turning up and down. The conversation keeps unraveling in a maze, until Anis' hand suddenly remembers the wine.

7

Half of the night and the wine, consumed by Anis and the guy. The conversations and the laughter have slowed down, the hands and the hearts of Anis and the guy, closer. The guy's poetry and story readings for Anis' smiles. The guy reads poems and stories in which their word order results in sound, but not any random perverse sound. That is why the choice of texts entails a particular pickiness; one has a choice of the classics and the contemporaries, or either.

We just need to keep in mind that the guy has to read texts which transform the wine in Anis' mouth, before it comes to a drop, to the shape of words.

After the first bottle confesses to the paleness of its wine, we no longer see that in the darkness of the early evening, the guy's hand has turned into an eye around Anis' shoulders, and Anis' head, a heart on the guy's chest. We only hear that they both have lied down tightly next to each other, as if because of cold or an unknown fear. The sound of feet and heartbeats. The sound of hands, eyes. The sound of lethargy.

8

We hear that Anis' voice becomes anxious, thinking that she wouldn't find an editing job. Her voice thinks that Mozdarani has become bitter with her and deliberately harasses her. Here, Anis' voice starts her anxious monologue. The short monologue is composed as such that the reader neither feels tired nor, due to its brevity, realizes that Mozdarani had an eye for her, and Anis' hand which branded a "No!" on his face. Also, it is necessary that the monologue include the fact that Mozdarani had Anis work mercilessly, so that he himself would work less, and even gave her petty errands, not editing jobs as if he wanted to deliberately harass her. We know that, until the day Anis left, nothing other than a few short conversations occurred between Anis and the guy. In the last moment, an old desire had been rekindled in Anis and the guy's veins, and Anis had not hesitated and suggested that they go to the cafe. The guy had first thought that Mozdarani was going to come with them, and had hesitated, but then a bit later, he had realized that Anis was trying to get rid of Mozdarani, and of course, with a bit of frankness, she made Mozdarani understand that she was going to go out only with the guy. When Mozdarani's eyes fall on the guy, he becomes infuriated, but doesn't show anything.

Monologues are usually boring, even the short ones. That is why it is preferred that we use sounds which Anis and the guy hear during Anis' monologue at the guy's home. From the sound of wind knocking on the windows, to the sound of the heater and the old fridge. Anis' monologue is left unfinished at the guy's kiss on her forehead; tomorrow they would go mountain-climbing and they have not slept yet.

9

Anis and the guy's lips, embraced by the mountain, repeating the taste of wine all the way, white the yellow of the air stands above their head, and now the sound of their shoes' friction, slowly and softly touching the rocks, as they are coming down the mountain, should be heard.

Every now and then, their hands are joined so that the other one wouldn't slip; the warmth of their lips has turned the snow on the mountain tops to the swishing of the water running under their feet. The path changes character with the voice of Anis and the guy, as if it has no borders, or if it does, it is soundless and does not warn.

As a result of frequent smoking, the guy's lungs, alternating between the time and the steepness, as was the case while climbing up, are ruined on every rock and its wheezing spreads out silver in the air. Anis' hand, disturbed, holds the guy's shoulders and silently listens to the scattered sliver in the air.

After they pass the sound of the many restaurants all the way to the city, we no longer see Anis and the guy cheerfully plopping down in the cab seat, their eyes looking for food. Although invisible to us, we still hear the sound of a forest, where the hunters are looking for prey, sniffing everywhere. Anis' mouth wants the guy's old fridge; she wants to hug it and kiss it until it is seduced enough to open up its chest of food. The guy's eyebrows trace a prey on a street corner. The sound of the cab's brake overshadows the sound of other cars honking.

10

When the phone ringing gets on Anis' nerves, the secretary of the Publishing Company picks up the phone with an offensive exhale; she had been filing her nails, and there had come a pause, perhaps. Anis' voice pulls itself together and smilingly asks the secretary to put her through to the manager. The secretary casts a look at the index finger of her right hand, half-filed, twirled around the phone wire. Anis' voice further pulls herself together, so that her smile can be seen better in the eyes of the manager.

The manager's voice becomes surprised, hearing that Mozdarani has not offered an editing job to Anis yet. Anis' voice becomes imbued with surprise, too, noticing that the manager is uninformed. It is better here to dig into Anis' mind, because she assumes that the manager knew and pretended that he did not know, or it was originally his own order to Mozdarani not to give her any assignment and send her on a wild-goose chase. Then again, we return to Anis' voice on the phone, now fading, and the manager's voice, saying that he would inform Mozdarani to make phone calls and to assign her some job before going to Shiraz.

Anis' hand, along with the receiver, in a small room with a bunk bed, paces with her feet. The sound of Anis' eyelids opening and closing. Slowness of the sounds, the breaths. Occasional pauses and turnings of the head. In one of those blinks, suddenly, Anis' glance falls on the backpack. As she is approaching it, her cell phone starts ringing and Mozdarani's voice glares and roars that: "we have no editing jobs for now and we'll let you know when we have one." The sound of Anis' eyelids shutting.

11

The sound of Anis' headache in the morning of the street, when her hand parts with the guy's hand. The sound of sidewalk's crowdedness and Anis' hand fishing out her cell phone from her pocket to read a text message. The sound of slowing down and then, Anis pausing on the sidewalk. The sound of Anis looking around the sidewalk.

On the last night, Anis talks to the guy about Emad's text sent to her on that morning of her parting with the guy. Faramarz, apparently, had seen the friction of Anis and the guy's shoulders in that speed of the yellow or green cab he was riding in, and he had touched the color of their lips and eyes in that morning of the street. His patience had run out, and after months, he had texted Anis and had hurled a torrent of abuse at the guy. Anis had ignored him, but then, Faramarz who had talked on the phone with his friend, Mozdarani, after a few hours, had apparently discovered who the guy was and had texted Anis again. Anis had shut her eyes, stretched her legs on the bed, and had bent her knees again, remembering the sweet moments she had spent with Faramarz, but Anis' lips had dried up and her smile was stuck on her face. Anis' hand had picked up the receiver, out of the blue, and had called Mozdarani. Mozdarani's voice had quivered when he had got nervous to reply back to Anis and he had said that he had first called Faramarz, and then Anis' hand had furiously hung up. The sound of rustling and porosity in Anis' headache.

12

Anis' backpack glides on the bed, all the way to Anis' chin and then, her look. The sound of gliding may not matter in describing the setting, but we have to be careful about Anis' eyelids, opening and closing, specifically, the closing of the eyelids' Anis' not-seeings. At one with Anis' look, we see the small room and a bunk, Anis and the backpack now unzipped, and Anis' hand, as if eternally groping. Nothing comes out of the backpack, ever, Anis' eyes are closing, the lids less, more slowly. Night.

13

We hear that Anis' hand and the wine dance next to the guy's bookshelves. The sound of the last night. The sound of the guy sitting next to Anis and the hexagon table. The sound of Anis' hair, when she turns her head around to flash in the guy's eyes. The sound of water dripping, and the fridge. The sound of lips and cheeks. The sound of eyes.

The sound of Anis' shoulders which, in the eyes of the guy and the wine, cackles every now and then. The sound of chalices, one after the other. The sound of night. Last night.

The sound of eyelids in front of one another. The sound of time. The sound of the last chalice and the chocolate. The sound of Anis' body and the guy's, when they fall down on the bed together. The unceasing sound of night. The sound of lips nibbling. The sound of light running into the veins. The sound of breaths and the warmth of the wine flowing from mouth to mouth. Sound of body. Sound of last night.

14

The novel ends with the stairs of a passenger bus, coming to contact with Anis' shoes out of the blue. We have to be really careful here, in describing the period of time elapsed, as the shoes come to contact with each stair. In each contact, the sounds around the bus become more vibrant and speed up, but the contact itself is dim and slow. It doesn't hurt the ear. But we stay right here. There is much noise in the air, and we focus on the conversations between the passengers and the crew; most of the conversations are around the destination, when the bus would leave, and the passengers' luggage. From the last stair, where Anis' shoes twirl on to get to her seat, to where Anis' hands take off her backpack in order to push it in the storage compartment above her head, we do not see anything, not even her eyes scanning others as they are scuttling through the narrow aisle between the seats. We see the comfort of her body spreading against the seat. Registering the light inside the bus is of utmost importance here. The sounds, too... less important, though. Then, all is soaked in white.

Appendix Night) (again

Publication Company

The sound of the guy's puffs on the cigarette in the morning on the balcony of the Publication Company.

The sound of the kettle banging in his head. The sound of tea.

The sound of a glass breaking while being washed, penetrating the air of the Publication Company.

The sound of Mr. Mansour' shirt, when he addresses the secretary with a tone of command, with the aid of his hands moving around.

The sound of the Publishing Company's door squeaking; the sound of the manager's smile in the rooms.

The playful sound of the guy's eyes when he speaks with Anis on the phone.

The sound of the authors in the waiting room.

The frustrated sound of the secretary's phone wire which doesn't have a moment of peace.

The scattered sound of Afsaneh in different rooms. The sound of her scurrying. The sound of doors unceasingly opening and closing and the sound of Afsaneh' tongue restless between them.

The sound of Mozdarani's ears sharpening for every thing.

The sound of censorship. The sound of cackling. The sound of fury. The sound of manager's worry about the books being mutilated.

The sound of the guy's thumb sliding over the cell phone buttons.

The sound of lunch, when the kitchen is breathing in the crowdedness of people.

The sound of Anis when the guy shuts his eyes. Anis' sound. Anis' sound.

Afsaneh

1. One morning Afsaneh wakes up and looks at herself in the bathroom mirror, remembering that evening when Mozdarani had put his lips on her and other girls' cheeks, to congratulate Nowrooz... and she suddenly vomits.

2. Afsaneh lives alone and she is renting. She has her breakfast, listening to the classical music.

3. As excitement crept into Mozdarani's voice, the sound of his eyelids twitching calmed down. The doctor had told her that she was nervous and she should take care of herself. Afsaneh softened her voice, but didn't say anything. The excitement in the voice had stiffened and wouldn't come down; she was

expecting a statement, a word to come out from the other's mouth. Afsaneh' eyebrows became kind and felt pity.

4. "Mozdarani is telling lies, but he said he had received a call from them, saying with a smile that they would come two nights later to pick him up. They had made him understand, with a grin, that it would be better if he cleared the house from documents and everything else. He said that on that night he had not been able to sleep, tossing and turning in his bed, till half past five in the morning, making the bed's springs sing in Fahimeh and their baby's ears. Fahimeh had put on her robe and her head scarf on the evening to be ready, in case they barged in the house.

"Not only they had not come in, but also they had respectfully asked him to come down. They had taken him into the car and had forced him not to open his eyes until they told him. He said he had realized from their voices that they were three. He had not dared open his eyes.

"They enter a building and they go up in the elevator, along with those three voices, and then the one on whom he is leaning takes him into a room and forces him to open his eyes and sit on the chair. He said that he heard the breathing sound of one of those three under his earlobes, and then, all of a sudden, the man's scream hurts his eardrum. Then, next to his other ear, the sound of the other one breathing is added.

He said that the first earlobe was still shocked by the dizziness of the scream.

"At last, one of those three would speak up, making him understand that his actions were against national security. But what actions?

"In short, he said that after a few hours of shouting and threatening, they had again taken him into the car and then they had asked him to get out around the Publication Company, and to count to fifty, and then, to open his eyes."

5. Afsaneh is sensitive to the sweat and the smell of people. They disgust her. During summers, Mozdarani's stinking body drives her crazy, but for a moment, she feels sorry for him.

6. Once, in the demonstrations after the election, Afsaneh was beaten black and blue. Afterwards, she was overpowered by insomnia.

Mr. Mansoor

1. At lunch time, all Mozdarani and Mr. Mansour eat is salad. They are both large-framed and fat; the only difference is that Mr. Mansour has short arms and almost no neck. That's why he always wears a wide-collared shirt. The sound of his fork gets to the bottom of the salad plate, and you can hear that from waist up, his heaviness of his shadow has fallen on the plate.

2. After Mr. Mansour bankrupted a pencil factory under his own management, and swindled all the money deceitfully, he returned to his old partner in the Publication and he became the financial and sales manager of the Publication.

3. Mr. Mansour always summarizes his obsessive compulsive disorder in the sound of water tap and washing hands.

4. "I totally believe in pigeon's shit. Once, I was supposed to sign a contract with a company for exporting stuff. I was hesitating. I started walking to the appointment. On the way, all of a sudden, some bird shit fell down in front of me. I did not hesitate. I returned home and cancelled the appointment. Afterwards, the editing staff realized how wisely I had decided."

5. Every morning, Mozdarani sniffs around the Publication to feel when Mr. Mansour' cologne is in the air. Every evening, when it is time to go, it is the sound of their farewell handshake which quivers the stairway of the Publication building.

6. Mr. Mansour after the suppression of post-election demonstrations had a stroke when he was descending the stairs of the Publication along with Mozdarani. Afterwards, he was overpowered by insomnia and ended up staying home.

A door
which is
turned
[like a
[page

So that terror disappears from my face

A Conversation with Mehdi Navid

Greetings friend! Thank you for talking to us about your process today! Can you introduce yourself, in a way that you would choose?

I was born in 1981 in Kermanshah, Iran. I am based in Tehran, Iran. I have worked for about twenty years as an author, translator and editor. My works include a collection of poetry in Persian titled ی دمای ن وت دم آ ب ش رس وت ی اج / م اگ ن ه ب [*You Didn't Arrive in Time / Dusk Fell Instead*] published by Bon-Gah publications, an unpublished novella, اه ن دب و اه ی رطب [*Bottles and Bodies*] and an unpublished novelette ت اوص ا ب ات ک [*The Book of Sounds*]. I have also translated numerous works from Samuel Beckett, Richard Brautigan and William S. Burroughs to Farsi. I worked as literary general editor for Ney Publication Company, and Rokhdad-e-NoPublication House. I also worked as a journalist for Karnameh Magazine. Currently, I am editor-in-chief of Pagard Publications.

Why are you a poet/writer/artist?

Everyone belongs to a certain class in society and his/her life is prone to certain events which determine their path in life; I am not an exception to this rule.

When did you decide you were a poet/writer/artist (and/or: do you feel comfortable calling yourself a poet/writer/artist, what other titles or affiliations do you prefer/feel are more accurate)?

I think I was sixteen or seventeen when the density of literature riveted its significance in my life. Everybody has their voice in this world and has their means to express it. Literature has always been the means by which I express myself. It is better to say that literature was a means by which terror disappeared from my face.

What's a "poet" (or "writer" or "artist") anyway?

Defining this is contingent on the circumstances; the artist, author or poet's estimation of their job varies depending on the time and the place they are in.It is always in transformation.

What do you see as your cultural and social role (in the literary / artistic /creative community and beyond)?

I mentioned before that I write so that terror

disappears from my face. Literature in the first place is contingent on the individual, and after the author is done working it can be contingent on the society, of course if others are able to communicate with the work. Then we can investigate to see whether that text (and not its author) has the potential to take on a socio-cultural role or not (and the perspective from which we view the socio-cultural role is by all means important).

Talk about the process or instinct to move this project into a body of work. How and why did this happen? Have you had this intention for a while? What encouraged and/or confounded this (or a book, in general) coming together? Was it a struggle?

I do not know how it happens. I mean I have not thought about it. Each time it has a different form and method. It is the beginning which matters; it is the point of reliance. For instance, when I write a poem a conception or disposition takes over my mind that reaches its destination once it settles. But when for instance I intend to write fiction-since it has a different form-I arrange the plot beforehand, however that plot is marginalized in the process of writing and the text takes on a whole new angle. I usually do not change the text much; I do not have a first, second, third draft. Everything must mount on one another brick by brick in a very orderly fashion so that the wall is built.

What formal structures or other constrictive practices (if any) do you use in the creation of your work? Have certain teachers or instructive environments, or readings/writings/work of other creative people informed the way you work/write?

Maybe it would be more accurate to talk about my strategy in writing that to say what or who inspired the structural form or the content of my work.

For me each work depending on its material circumstances defines its own structure. And naturally this type of approach stems from my lives experience. It is better to say that my work is a kind of experimental work; it is not a trial and error kind of thing, it is not right or wrong, it is a matter of borders, a border which it creates by itself, quite like our life which describes its border and proceeds on the edge.

The work itself decides what form it is going to take on to express itself, what parts it is going to put on display more conspicuously and what parts to keep in the shadow. As a result, the structural form and the content of each work, in my opinion, emanates from the lived experience of the author or artist and their circumstances.

Speaking of monikers, what does your title represent? How was it generated? Talk about the way you titled the book, and how your process of naming (individual pieces, sections, etc) influences you and/or colors your work specifically.

The title of *The Book of Sounds* refers to the work I have done in the text; a struggle to create sounds in the texture of the text. I intended to make the reader hear the sounds in their mind's ear and thence approach the text.

What does this particular work represent to you as indicative of your method/creative practice, history, mission/intentions/hopes/plans?

The Book of Sounds specifically intends to build a tangible whole by means of insignificant, trivial and marginal details-which are not usually deemed significant in typical fiction-this is its fictional universe; by means of sounds, by means of personification of objects, dispositions and atmosphere, etc.

What would be the best possible outcome for this book? What might it do in the world, and how will its presence as an object facilitate your creative role in your community and beyond? What are your hopes for this book, and for your practice?

I hope this works is seen and read and I hope I will be able to get feedback from the readers. This book is a microcosm of the contemporary Iranian fictional literature which is kind of a minority in today's world literature.

Let's talk a little bit about the role of poetics and creative community in social activism, in particular in what I call 'Civil Rights 2.0,' which has remained immediately present all around us in the time leading up to this publication. I'd be curious to hear some thoughts on the challenges we face in speaking and publishing across lines of race, age, privilege, social/cultural background, and sexuality within the community, vs. the dangers of remaining and producing in isolated 'silos.'

Unfortunately what is ignored in social activism and entraps it into a vicious circle is ignorance about the pertinent forces in the historical and geographical state of affairs and depleting it of the political precept (especially in developing countries). Transcribing social activism in one society and implementing it in another is indicative of ignorance about the potential, possibilities and pertinent forces in that society (which is what we are witnessing in developing countries). Or a social activity insists on repeating itself so much that it becomes threadbare and is not compatible with the circumstances of the society anymore.

But I believe that creative work goes beyond sociopolitical activism; it is unequaled. And it is the collectivity of the creative works that makes the societal atmosphere seethe. Before the formation of movements against racial, gender and class discrimination, the creative and unequaled works of art were at the frontline in uniting minorities and affecting public opinion.

Thus, I think that the creative work should create gaps in the dominant order, it should make it problematic.

Mehdi Navid (b. 1981) is an Iranian author, translator and editor. His works include a collection of poetry in Persian titled تو نیامدی بهنگام / جای تو سر شب آمد [*You Didn't Arrive in Time / Dusk Fell Instead*] published by Bon-Gah publications, an unpublished novella, بطری‌ها و بدن‌ها [*Bottles and Bodies*] and an the novelette کتاب اصوات [*The Book of Sounds*]. He is currently working on two novellas, one concerning an infamous historical incident which occurred in Iran the 90s involving a number of Iranian authors and another on the assassination of secular intellectuals and writers in the mid- nineties, which is known as chain-murders. He has also translated numerous works from Samuel Beckett, Richard Brautigan and William S. Burroughs to Farsi. He worked as literary general editor for Ney Publication Company, and Rokhdad-e-No Publication House. He also worked as a journalist for Karnameh Magazine. Currently, he is editor-in-chief of Pagard Publications.

Reflections

Ashkan Eslami Fard

It took me a while. I have not even noticed that I missed this place. The last touch of my feet with these sidewalks under a sky so heavy with clouds was three years and a summer ago. Then, I had not yet known that I would miss the objects and scents and sounds and people. But the nostalgia began to spill drop by drop, its heavy fragrance a flavor to every second of every minute of every hour. It encompassed my life. It happened in an aura of awe of skyscrapers and bridges; An ocean of metal, greed, nudity, and their reflections in the water. It took me a while to notice the little details I have been longing for.

The lower side of Southern Bahar street runs all the way down Enghelab Ave. It passes intersections and fruit stores and donuts and flies in window shops and it ends in a chaotic mess of cars turning all the way to the left before making a U-turn from the rightmost side of the eastbound lanes of the avenue bisected by the curb that runs along and under the middle lane that then elevates to an overpass. This is the network, the infinite loop of desire and chase for money, for brain, for flesh. The taxis know where to hunt for passengers without getting honked at.

This southern neighborhood of the town has been around for a while before the city crept outwards toward all that was left of green hillsides that sprawled beneath the mountains, where the streets are steep and the rainwater runs through brooks in streams. This part is rather flat. The rain stays where it lands only to reflect inverted shadows of people and the green and the yellow of taxis and the red of the traffic lights. What it doesn't reflect is the rushing of street-side vendors sheltering their cheap papers and books from the wet that crawls under the tablecloth on which they put them and meet the paper to turn thoughts into paste. These vendors always do that when the sun smiles at them for if they don't, there will be nothing but bread on the table tonight. Neither does it reflect the occasional cluster of students straight out of school around a cart of cheap street food that fills the stomach but not the brain. The food is cheap because if it is not, it is not sold at all. This neighborhood revolves around the interdependence of the lives of these students and that of those who feed their minds and stomachs, a byproduct of which is the copious number of books and many publication offices and those who wander in and out of them.

In the next few miles the products of thoughts dominate; only those that have passed through filters and offices and rooms and hands moist with sweat, on the second and third floors of brick buildings that cower behind their contemporary composite contemporaries, lest they don't get demolished and replace by the ones that stood by the streets. Composite was an idiosyncrasy of the new era. And such is it that sometimes those who have the temerity to stay their ground get demolished. On my way my eyes hang onto a dusty window shop and then another. I suddenly identify the elongated orthogonal fonts from a few decades ago. Before I was born. Then I suddenly know the dust that has penetrated the glass. It speaks to me the language of nostalgia. I remember the years I lived vicariously through the warm voice of my father as it shook when we drove past them. It took me a while to hear. It took the voice three years and summer to permeate past my mind in a box where feelings hide, right where another "I" lives through a green or yellow taxi, through the red reflection of a traffic light lit in a halo of rainwater as it eavesdrops on the voices of vendors fading into that of wetness on the asphalt, amplified by the rush of feet towards yellow and green shelters. Their stomachs are full tonight. Now these distant lights are a reminder of the time when the darkness spilled in, and in it I could see the very lit dots. I was landing in Boston. These taxis remind me of my tongue that stuttered in a taxi whose driver's Boston accent I could barely understand. It took my eyes a while and a thousand miles to look into the darkness I have always avoided, only to find the light in its winter slumber. It took me a while to learn the language of chosen displacement that stuffed my throat with silence at times. The silence that strikes me as I walk on this pavement. I can hear it through the chaos and noise and the melancholy of colors on advertising placards:

theses,
projects,
final papers for sale,
I can hear it speak freedom from under shawls and gowns.

This part of the town reminds me of the reflection of lit windows of towers that reach out for the sky, where life is restrained in containers and walls are built around properties and objects and people. I walk down Myrtle Ave. towards the low ceiling that shelters me from the burden of the sky hanging massively above. I'm stuck in a past that cannot find its way to this world ofsounds until right after I realized that even if it did, nobody in this vicinity would understand it. It would not go beyond eardrums because nobody in this vicinity speaks it. I should have gone back and searched that voice among reflections and shouts and honks and rain. But I chose to stay, and much of it got shaved off. It took my ears three years and a summer to hear the chirping of the larks, to notice the dust on the window shops and the bookstores and publications, to see the walking, the wandering of people in and out of rooms, to notice the touches of hands, to see the smile in eyes, to hear the leakage of thoughts onto sidewalks and papers. Now I hear mine too. Only now I know that I have found it. The sounds are waiting for me to go back. It took me a while.

TINA RAHIMI (translator) is an Iranian teacher, writer, and translator. She received her MA in English Language and Literature from Allameh Tabataba'i University in 2005, and her PhD in Media and Communication from the European Graduate School in 2013. She has worked as a writera nd content-creator for language companies such as Living Language and Rosetta Stone. She has taught Farsi to students from around the world and has also participated in translation projects such as "Seeing Studies" by Documenta 13. She has translated articles by contemporary philosophers such as Slavoj Žižek and Judith Butler, poems by John Keats, and a short story by Jorge Luis Borges. She currently lives in Madrid, Spain.

ASHKAN ESLAMI FARD (asst. translator/ asst. editor) I am Ashkan. I was born in 35.6892° N, 51.3890° E, Earth. I'm 22 years old, and I left to the US when I was 19 to let another environment shape the rest of me. I'm enthusiastic about the power of language, and a speaker of Farsi, French, English, some Turkish and some german. Through these years of studying different languages and interacting with speakers of these languages I have come to understand the tragic reality of things that get lost in translation; the delicate coming-together of sounds and ideas that can only exist in one realm and perish once they are put into another. Beyond that, I have sympathetically observed amazing minds being hampered by their inability to use languages that do not have the privilege of being used by a majority of people. Therefore, part of my contribution is to try my best to help these minds, thoughts, and ideas translate over. I have been blessed to work with the Operating System and the extraordinarily thoughtful minds behind it.

Why Print / Document?

*he Operating System uses the language "print document" to differentiate from the book-bject as part of our mission to distinguish the act of documentation-in-book-FORM om the act of publishing as a backwards-facing replication of the book's agentive *role* s it may have appeared the last several centuries of its history. Ultimately, I approach the ook as TECHNOLOGY: one of a variety of printed documents (in this case,* bound*) that umans have invented and in turn used to archive and disseminate ideas, beliefs, stories, nd other evidence of production.*

wnership and use of printing presses and access to (or restriction of printed materials) has ng been a site of struggle, related in many ways to revolutionary activity and the fight for vil rights and free speech all over the world. While (in many countries) the contemporary uotidian landscape has indeed drastically shifted in its access to platforms for sharing formation and in the widespread ability to "publish" digitally, even with extremely limited sources, the importance of publication on physical media has not diminished. In ct, this may be the most critical time in recent history for activist groups, artists, and thers to insist upon learning, establishing, and encouraging personal and community ocumentation practices. Hear me out.

Vith The OS's print endeavors I wanted to open up a conversation about this: the ltimately radical, transgressive act of creating PRINT /DOCUMENTATION in the igital age. It's a question of the archive, and of history: who gets to tell the story, and hat evidence of our life, our behaviors, our experiences are we leaving behind? We an know little to nothing about the future into which we're leaving an unprecedentedly igital document trail — but we can be assured that publications, government agencies, useums, schools, and other institutional powers that be will continue to leave BOTH a igital and print version of their production for the official record. Will we?

s a (rogue) anthropologist and long time academic, I can easily pull up many accounts bout how lives, behaviors, experiences — how THE STORY of a time or place — was ieced together using the deep study of correspondence, notebooks, and other physical ocuments which are no longer the norm in many lives and practices. As we move our reative behaviors towards digital note taking, and even audio and video, what can e predict about future technology that is in any way assuring that our stories will be ccurately told – or told at all? How will we leave these things for the record?

n these documents we say:
VE WERE HERE, WE EXISTED, WE HAVE A DIFFERENT STORY

- ELAE [Lynne DeSilva-Johnson], Founder/Creative Director
THE OPERATING SYSTEM, Brooklyn NY 2017

Glossarium: Unsilenced Texts

The Operating System's *Glossarium: Unsilenced Texts* series was established in early 2016 in an effort to recover silenced voices outside and beyond the canon, seeking out and publishing both contemporary translations and little or un-known out of print texts, in particular those under siege by restrictive regimes and silencing practices in their home (or adoptive) countries. We are committed to producing dual-language versions whenever possible.

The term "Glossarium" derives from latin/greek and is defined as "a collection of glosses or explanations of words, especially of words not in general use, as those of a dialect, locality or an art or science, or of particular words used by an old or a foreign author." The series is curated by OS Founder and Managing Editor Lynne DeSilva-Johnson, with the help of global collaborators.

Other active and forthcoming titles in this series include:

*Ashraf Fayadh, *Instructions Within* (Arabic)
tr. Mona Kareem, Jonathan Wright, and Mona Zaki.
*Gregory Randall's award winning memoir of life in Cuba
To Have Been There Then (Estar Allí Entonces); tr. Margaret Randall
*Jerome Rothenberg and Harold Cohen, *Flower World Variations, Expanded Edition.* Translated from the Yaqui Deer Dances.
*Chely Lima, *Lo Que Les Dijo El Licántropo / What the Werewolf Told Them.* (Spanish), tr. Margaret Randall
**La Comandante Maya*, Rita Valdivia. (Spanish-English) tr. M. Randall.
*Israel Domínguez, *Viaje de Regreso / Return Trip,* (Spanish)
tr. Margaret Randall, with art by Jose Parla and JR.
*Marta Zelwan, *Śnienie / Dreaming* (Polish-English) tr. Victoria Miluch
*Hélène Sanguinetti, *Alparegho, Pareil-À-Rien / Alparegho, Like Nothing Else;* (French-English/dual-language), tr. Ann Cefola
*Bijan Elahi, *High Tide Of The Eyes* (Farsi); tr. Rebecca Ruth Gould and Kayvan Tahmasebian
*Sergio Loo, *Operation on a Malignant Body* (Spanish), tr. Will Stockton
*Katrin Ottarsdóttir, *Are There Copper Pipes in Heaven?* (Faroese),
tr. Matthew Landrum
**In the Drying Shed of Souls: Poetry from Cuba's Generation Zero*,
ed. Katherine Hedeen & Víctor Rodríguez Núñez
*Brent Armendinger, *Street Gloss;* [*feat.* Alejandro Méndez, Alejandro Méndez, Fabián Casas, Néstor Perlongher & Diana Bellessi; Spanish]

Additional Recent & Forthcoming Titles, 2018-19

Ark Hive-Marthe Reed
I Made for You a New Machine and All it Does is Hope - Richard Lucyshyn
Illusory Borders-Heidi Reszies
A Year of Misreading the Wildcats - Orchid Tierney
A Bony Framework for the Tangible Universe-D. Allen
Opera on TV-James Brunton
Hall of Waters-Berry Grass
Transitional Object-Adrian Silbernagel
We Are Never The Victims - Timothy DuWhite
Of Color: Poets' Ways of Making | An Anthology of Essays on Transformative Poetics
- Amanda Galvan Huynh & Luisa A. Igloria, Editors
An Absence So Great and Spontaneous It Is Evidence of Light - Anne Gorrick
The Book of Everyday Instruction - Chloë Bass
The Suitcase Tree - Filip Marinovich
Chlorosis - Michael Flatt and Derrick Mund
Sussuros a Mi Padre - Erick Sáenz
In Corpore Sano : Creative Practice and the Challenged Body [Anthology]
Abandoners - L. Ann Wheeler
Jazzercise is a Language - Gabriel Ojeda-Sague
Born Again - Ivy Johnson
Attendance - Rocío Carlos and Rachel McLeod Kaminer
Singing for Nothing - Wally Swist
The Ways of the Monster - Jay Besemer
A Field Guide to Autobiography - Melissa Eleftherion

DOC U MENT

/däkyəmənt/

First meant "instruction" or "evidence," whether written or not.

noun - a piece of written, printed, or electronic matter that provides information or evidence or that serves as an official record
verb - record (something) in written, photographic, or other form
synonyms - paper - deed - record - writing - act - instrument

[*Middle English, precept, from Old French, from Latin documentum, example, proof, from docre, to teach; see dek- in Indo-European roots.*]

Who is responsible for the manufacture of value?

Based on what supercilious ontology have we landed in a space where we vie against other creative people in vain pursuit of the fleeting credibilities of the scarcity economy, rather than freely collaborating and sharing openly with each other in ecstatic celebration of MAKING?

While we understand and acknowledge the economic pressures and fear-mongering that threatens to dominate and crush the creative impulse, we also believe that ***now more than ever we have the tools to relinquish agency via cooperative means,*** fueled by the fires of the Open Source Movement.

Looking out across the invisible vistas of that rhizomatic parallel country we can begin to see our community beyond constraints, in the place where intention meets resilient, proactive, collaborative organization.

Here is a document born of that belief, sown purely of imagination and will.
When we document we assert. We print to make real, to reify our being there.
When we do so with mindful intention to address our process, to open our work to others, to create beauty in words in space, to respect and acknowledge the strength of the page we now hold physical, a thing in our hand,
we remind ourselves that, like Dorothy: *we had the power all along, my dears.*

THE PRINT! DOCUMENT SERIES

is a project of

the trouble with bartleby

in collaboration with

the operating system

www.ingramcontent.com/pod-product-compliance
Lightning Source LLC
Chambersburg PA
CBHW070504170726
48291CB00008B/2655

* 9 7 8 1 9 4 6 0 3 1 2 9 7 *

کتابِ اصوات

مهدی نوید

کتابِ اصوات

مهدی نوید

برای طهورای صبح، ظهر و شب

در این چشم‌انداز بیش‌ترِ آدم‌ها قلابی‌اند. هر جور شباهت میانِ آن‌ها و کسانِ واقعی مایه تأسف کسانِ واقعی باید باشد.

ابراهیم گلستان

۱

رمان از پله‌های اتوبوسی مسافری آغاز می‌شود که کفش‌های انیس بی‌هوا روی‌شان به اصطکاک در می‌آید. باید حواس‌مان جمع باشد که فاصله‌ی زمانی برخوردِ کفش‌ها را با هر پله درست شرح دهیم. در هر اصطکاک صداهای اطرافِ اتوبوس پررنگ‌تر می‌شود و سرعت دارد، اما صدای خودِ اصطکاک کند و بم است؛ گوش را نمی‌خراشد. اما در این‌جا می‌مانیم. صداهای اطراف زیاد است و دقیق می‌شویم به گفت‌وگوهای کوتاهِ مسافران و خدمه‌ی اتوبوس؛ بیش‌ترِ حرف‌ها حولِ مقصدِ اتوبوس و زمانِ حرکت و بارهای مسافران می گردد. از پله‌ی آخری که کفش‌های انیس روی‌اش چرخی می‌خورد تا به صندلی‌اش برسد تا آن‌جا که دست‌های

انیس کوله‌پشتی‌اش را درمی‌آورد تا در بالای سرش جاسازی کند، هیچ نمی‌بینیم؛ حتا چشم‌هاش را که وقتِ گذر از راه‌باریکه‌ی بینِ صندلی‌ها دوان و چرخان به دیگران می‌افتد. ما آرامشِ تنش را می‌بینیم که لم داده بر صندلی. ثبتِ نورِ داخلِ اتوبوس در این‌جا اهمیتِ بسیار دارد. صداها هم، کم‌تر البته. بعد همه چیز در سفیدی فرو می‌رود.

کوله‌پشتیِ انیس سریده می‌شود روی تخت تا می‌رسد زیرِ چانه و بعدتر نگاهِ انیس. صدای سریده‌شدن شاید خیلی به ترسیمِ فضا کمکی نکند، اما حواس‌مان باشد که باز و بسته شدنِ پلك‌های انیس مهم است، به‌خصوص بسته‌شدنِ پلك‌ها... ندیدن‌های انیس. هم‌زمان با نگاهِ انیس، فضای کوچكِ اتاق را می‌بینیم و یك تختِ دو طبقه با انیس و کوله‌پشتی، که حالا دیگر زیپش باز شده و دستِ انیس که انگار کورمالی مدام است. چیزی از درونِ کوله‌پشتی بیرون نمی‌آید اصلاً، چشم‌های انیس بسته‌تر می‌شود، پلك‌ها کم‌تر، کُندتر. شب.

چشم‌های انیس در اواخرِ ظهری سرد پیِ آدم‌ها و دیوارها می گردد. قرار است برود داخلِ ساختمانِ انتشارات. کتابی ویرایش کرده انیس.

دست‌های انیس در اتاقِ مدیرِ انتشارات غیر از این که حرف بزنند کارِ دیگری ندارند. دهانِ مدیر را نمی‌بینیم، فقط می‌شنویم که خوشحال است و سرِحال از دیدنِ انیس. گفت‌وگویی کوتاه شکل می گیرد بین‌شان درباره‌ی کار. لب‌های انیس حینِ گفت‌وگو آرام بی قرارِ جایی دیگر است. گفت‌وگو هرچند کوتاه است اما باید طوری نوشته شود که احساسِ کندی و آهستگی را القاء کند؛ به هیچ عنوان فضا سرد نیست فقط بی‌قراری و انتظار است که باید خوب ترسیم شود.

صدای جیرجیرِ در وقتی پاهای انیس خروج می کنند.

(به‌نظر می‌رسد که محلِ ساختمانِ انتشارات مهم باشد، مخصوصاً برای صحنه‌های بعدتر: انتشارات واقع است در جلوی پلی بزرگ و ماشین‌رو. زیرش چند کتاب‌فروشی است و درواقع یک‌جورهایی راسته‌ی کتاب‌فروشی‌ها را شکل داده است. ساختمانی که انتشارات در آن است قدیمی است و انتشارات در طبقه‌ی دومِ آن سکنا گزیده. پله‌های راه‌پله از سنگ‌های متخلخل تشکیل شده و همچنان هویتِ قدیمی‌اش را حفظ کرده. اما درِ انتشارات و فضای داخلیِ آن بویی از قدمت نبرده، همه چیز نونوار است: از رنگِ دیوارها گرفته تا میز و صندلی‌ها، و حتا کرکره‌ها و پنجره‌ها. تنها چیزی که در فضای مدرنِ انتشارات ممکن است خودنمایی کند صدای جیرجیرِ درهاست. اما انگار این صدا آزارنده نیست، و گرنه حتماً روغن‌کاری می‌شد لولاها.)

قدم‌های شلِ انیس وقتی واردِ اتاقِ ویرایش می‌شود، باید طوری بنماید که خواننده بفهمد انیس پیش از این یک هفته‌یی در این اتاق کار کرده و بعد از آن متوجه شده که در این‌جا نیروش هرز می‌رود و به کارهاش دیگر نمی‌رسد. و همین شده که انیس از انتشارات زده بیرون و بهانه‌یی جور کرده برای مدیر و گفته پدرش ازش خواسته برگردد شیراز پیشِ خودش و حالا که درسش تمام شده نمی‌خواهد دیگر کار کند. مدیر هم این وسط سعی کرده دلداری بدهد انیس را و گفته هر چه پدرت می‌گوید گوش بگیر، چون صلاحت را می‌خواهد. اما همین‌قدر هم می‌دانیم که انیس به پولِ این کار احتیاج داشته و البته دوست داشته در تهران بماند و به

کارهای خودش برسد: نوشتن. به هر حال، انیس برمی گردد شیراز و از انتشارات کارِ ویرایشِ کتاب می گیرد تا گذرانِ زند گی کند و بعد هم برسد به کارهای خودش.

قدم‌های شلِ انیس وقتی واردِ اتاقِ ویرایش می‌شود، آقای مزدرانی از جاش برمی‌خیزد و با خنده‌یی می‌پرسد سوغاتی چه آورده است، بی‌سلام. دست‌های انیس کشیده می‌شود روی سطحِ صافِ میزِ چوبی‌یی که یك هفته‌یی پشتش کار کرده است و بعد نشیمنگاهِ انیس که خودش را روی صندلیِ پشتِ میز جا می‌دهد. و لب‌های خشكِ انیس به‌همراهیِ دستش که دیگر از روی سطحِ میز بلند شده می گویند که فقط برای مدیر مسقطی آورده‌اند. مزدرانی انگار که بهش برخورده باشد از اتاق خارج می‌شود و پیشِ مدیر می‌رود و جعبه‌ی مسقطی را برمی‌دارد؛ احتمالاً به این بهانه که به همه‌ی بچه‌های انتشارات تعارف کند. و همین کار را هم می کند. بعد برمی گردد پیشِ انیس با مسقطی، اما تعارفش نمی کند. چشم‌های انیس از این حرکتِ مزدرانی که مسقطی را از مدیر گرفته جا می‌خورد و در انتهای حدقه می‌ماند، اما لب‌های انیس پیِ جایی دیگر است و از این رو بحثِ گرفتنِ کارِ بعدی را برای ویرایش پیش می کشند تا زودتر از این فضا جان به در برند.

مزدرانی لب‌های کلفتی دارد، اما وقتی حرف می‌زند انگار از تنبلی خیلی تکان نمی‌خورد، یعنی دیده نمی‌شود. فقط چینِ صورت و چشم‌هاش است که خون درشان دویده می‌شود. گوش‌های انیس متوجه می‌شوند که قرار نیست کارِ بعدی را به او بدهد، چون همه چیز را به آینده موکول می‌کند مزدرانی. چشم‌های انیس پیِ صدای کلاغی‌ست که درست پشتِ سرِ مزدرانی در آن‌سویِ پنجره روی درخت نشسته است. تُنِ صدای مزدرانی بلند است اما انیس می‌داند که چشم‌هاش باید به همین صدای کلاغ دلخوش باشند تا وقت بگذرد.

باید این را نیز مدِ نظر قرار دهیم که هنگامِ روایتِ این صحنه پسری هم وارد ماجرا می‌شود: هم‌اویی که لب‌های انیس بی‌قرارش است. بهتر است در لحظه‌یی که مزدرانی برای گرفتنِ جعبه‌ی مسقطی پیشِ مدیر می‌رود، انیس نیز به آشپزخانه برود، و از قضا پسر را در حالِ کشیدنِ سیگار در بالکنِ آشپزخانه ببیند. در خلوت و سکوتِ آشپزخانه لحظه‌یی لب‌های هر دوشان حلقه‌یی می‌شود دورِ گردن و شانه‌های هم. گونه‌های انیس به‌ناگهان، انگار یادِ چیزی افتاده باشد، همراهِ باقیِ چهره‌اش یك لحظه می‌گردد تا دست‌های انیس شرابی را که از شیراز برای پسر به‌همراه داشته از اتاقِ ویرایش بیاورد.

مزدرانی در این حین هنوز در حالِ تعارفِ مسقطی به دیگر همکاران است، اما گوش‌هاش می‌بیند که دست‌های انیس سرخوش کیسه‌یی نقره‌یی را به آشپزخانه می‌برند و چندی بعد خالی و رها به اتاقِ ویرایش بازمی گردند و پشت‌بندش پسر با همان خش‌خشِ نقره‌یی از آشپزخانه بیرون می آید.

چشم‌های انیس وقتی دست در دستِ پسر از راه‌پله‌ی انتشارات پایین می‌آید. شانه‌های انیس و پسر که سایشی آرام دارد موقعِ دور زدن از پاگرد. قدم‌هاشان که روی هوا صدای شادی می‌پراکند؛ کفش‌ها از روی پله‌ها می‌جهند انگار.

صحنه جوری چیده شده است که وقتی پاهای انیس و پسر از آستانه‌ی درِ ساختمانِ انتشارات می‌گذرند، می‌دانیم که قرار است بی‌هیچ لختی به‌سمتِ خانه‌ی پسر بروند، برای همین درنگی در جلوی در جایز نیست. از این‌جا دیگر نمی‌بینیم که انیس و پسر که حالا قدم‌هاشان کندتر از قبل شده چه‌طور از خیابانِ منتهی به خانه‌ی پسر پیاده می‌روند و برای شب‌شان خرید می‌کنند، اما بد نیست گذری سریع بر سر و صداهای خیابان بکنیم و تاکسی‌هایی را شرح دهیم که پر تعدادند و پیِ

مسافر می‌چرخند و به‌طورِ حتم وقتی از کنارِ مغازه‌های صنایعِ دستی و شیرینی‌فروشی و سوپرمارکت‌ها می‌گذرند، رنگِ زرد یا سبزِ بدنه‌شان لحظه‌یی، هر چند کوتاه، با دست‌های درهم‌چفتِ انیس و پسر که از پیاده‌رو پایین می‌روند برخورد داشته. حواس‌مان باشد که در این گذرِ سریع احتیاجی به صداهای آدم‌های خیابان نداریم، حتا صدای راننده‌های تاکسی که از سر و کولِ مسافر بالا می‌روند.

همچنان نمی‌بینیم که انیس و پسر خریدشان را کرده‌اند و حتا پسر انیس را از کوچه‌پس‌کوچه‌هایی برده تا خانه‌هایی را نشانش دهد که معماریِ قدیمی و زیباشان دل می‌برند. انیس این میان دل داده به خانه‌ها، اما به خنده اشاره کرده به شیراز و پسر هم فهمیده زیره برده است به کرمان انگار. بعد هر دو خندیده‌اند و دستِ انیس دوباره نگاه کرده به دستِ پسر و به آنی قاپیده‌اش.

۶

صدای کلیدی که در قفل می‌چرخد و بعد صدای کفش‌های پسر که وارد می‌شود و به‌دنبالش چشم‌های انیس که پیِ نوای فضای خانه لحظه‌یی گوش می‌ایستد، و بعد لبخندِ انیس که رنگ می‌اندازد به کتاب‌های داخلِ کتابخانه‌ی پسر. پسر تا این موقع لباس‌هاش را در تنها اتاق‌خوابِ خانه عوض کرده و بر گشته پیشِ نگاهِ انیس. پاهای انیس راهِ اتاق‌خواب را گرفته و رفته، بعد بر گشته، بی‌جوراب آمده نشسته روی مبلِ سه‌نفره، کنارِ پسر.

از این‌جا تا زمانی که دستِ انیس بی‌هوا یادِ شراب می‌افتد، گفت‌و گو یی بین‌شان درمی گیرد. این گفت‌و گو ظرافتی خاص می‌طلبد، چون هم حولِ ادبیات می گردد و هم وضعیتِ زند گی‌شان؛ انگار دو نفر برای اولین‌بار نشسته‌اند

کنارِ هم و می‌خواهند در کسری از ثانیه همه چیز را بریزند روی دایره. اما پیچیدگیِ این گفت‌وگو ظرافتی دیگر را نیز فرامی‌خواند: هر دو به‌اندازه‌ی کافی انگار هم را می‌شناسند، انگار سال‌هاست این دوستی قدمت دارد. خواننده البته متوجه است که در واقعیت چنین نیست، بلکه این اشتراکاتِ زیستی است که این دو را در هم بر زده است.

از مهم‌ترین نکات برای آرایشِ گفت‌وگو بازی با حالتِ دست‌های انیس و شیوه‌ی نشستنِ پسر است، و البته میزی کوتاه و هشت‌گوش اما بزرگ، و تلاقیِ صدای ورق‌خوردنِ کتاب‌هایی که از کتابخانه بیرون آورده می‌شود و صدای پلکِ چشم‌ها. ما در این‌جا صدای تلفنِ همراهِ انیس را که چند باری زنگ می‌خورد نمی‌شنویم، حتا صدای هرازگاهِ تلویزیون را که پسر کم و زیاد می‌کند. گفت‌وگو در دالانی پیچاپیچ به راه خود می‌رود تا دستِ انیس بی‌هوا یادِ شراب بیفتد.

نصفِ شراب و شب صرفِ انیس و پسر. گفت‌وگوها و خنده‌ها کندتر شده، دست و دلِ انیس و پسر نزدیک‌تر. شعر و داستان خواندن‌های پسر برای لبخندهای انیس. پسر شعر و داستان‌هایی می‌خواند که می‌داند شکلِ قرارگیریِ کلمه‌هاشان در امتدادِ هم تولیدِ صوت می‌کند، اما نه هر صوتِ کژ و کوژی. برای همین، انتخابِ متون برای این قطعه وسواسی عجیب می‌طلبد؛ هم از کلاسیک‌ها می‌توان آورد و هم از معاصرها، و یا فقط از یکی‌شان. فقط حواس‌مان باشد متن‌هایی را پسر بخواند که شرابِ در دهانِ انیس را، پیش از آن‌که به جرعه برسد، شکلِ کلمه‌ها کند.

بطرِ اول که به محویِ شرابش اعتراف کند، دیگر نمی‌بینیم که در تاریکیِ اواخرِ شب دستِ پسر چشمی شده دورِ

شانه‌های انیس، و سرِ انیس قلبی بر سینه‌ی پسر. فقط می‌شنویم که هر دو دراز کشیده‌اند چفتاچفتِ هم، انگار از سرما یا ترسی نامعلوم. صدای پاها و ضربانِ قلب‌ها. صدای دست‌ها، چشم‌ها. صدای لختی.

می‌شنویم که صدای انیس نگران می‌شود از این که دیگر نتواند کار برای ویرایش بگیرد. صداش فکر می کند که مزدرانی با او چپ افتاده است و عمداً اذیتش می کند. در این‌جا صدای انیس تک گوییِ نگرانِ خود را می آغازد. تک گویی طوری تنظیم شود که خواننده نه احساسِ خستگی کند و نه از فرطِ کوتاهی متوجه شود مزدرانی به انیس نظر داشته و دستِ انیس که مُهرِ مردودی را بر صورتِ او داغ کرده. همین‌طور، در تک گویی آورده شود که مزدرانی انیس را در آن یك هفته به هر جور بیگاری واداشته تا خودش کم‌تر کار کند و حتا بیش‌تر کارِ گل به او می‌داده تا کارِ ویرایش، انگار به عمد می‌خواسته اذیتش کند. می‌دانیم که بینِ انیس و پسر تا روزِ وداعِ انیس به‌جز چند مکالمه‌ی کوتاه

و معمولی اتفاقِ دیگری نیفتاده. انیس و پسر در آن دمِ آخر هوسی قدیمی در رگ‌هاشان سر خورده و انیس هم معطلش نکرده و به پسر پیشنهاد داده بروند کافه. پسر اول فکر کرده قرار است مزدرانی هم همراه‌شان بیاید و دست‌دست کرده، اما کمی بعد متوجه شده که انیس دارد مزدرانی را دست‌به‌سر می‌کند و البته با کمی صراحت متوجه‌اش می‌کند که قرار است فقط با پسر بیرون برود. چشم‌های مزدرانی که به پسر می‌افتد لجش می‌گیرد، اما چیزی نشان نمی‌دهد.

تک‌گوییِ معمولاً خسته‌کننده است، حتا کوتاهش.

برای همین ترجیح دارد از اصواتی استفاده کنیم که انیس و پسر در هنگامِ تک‌گوییِ انیس در خانه‌ی پسر می‌شنوند. از صدای باد گرفته که به پنجره‌ها می‌خورد تا صدای بخاری و یخچالِ قدیمی. تک‌گوییِ انیس نیمه‌کاره رها می‌شود با بوسه‌ی پسر بر پیشانیِ انیس؛ فردا می‌خواهند بروند کوه و هنوز نخوابیده‌اند.

۹

لب‌های انیس و پسر که در پناهِ کوه طعمِ شرابِ طولِ راه را به تکرار بگیرند، زرده‌ی هوا بالا سرشان ایستاده و دیگر باید صدای پایینِ آمدنِ اصطکاکِ کفش‌هاشان را از کوه شنید که آهسته و نرم بر سنگ‌ها می‌خورد. هرازگاه دست‌هاشان به‌هم می‌پیوندد تا آن یکی سُر نخورد؛ گرمیِ لب‌هاشان برفِ نشسته بر کوه را به شُرشُرِ آبی بدل کرده که از زیرِ پاشان دوان است. راه با صدای انیس و پسر تغییرِ رفتار می‌دهد، مرز ندارد انگار، یا اگر دارد بی‌صداست و هشدار نمی‌دهد. سینه‌ی پسر از سیگارِ زیاد به تناوبِ زمان و شیب، همچون وقتِ بالا آمدن، خراب می‌شود روی هر تخته‌سنگی و خس‌خسش نقره می‌پراکند در هوا. دستِ انیس نگرانِ شانه‌ی پسر را می‌گیرد و صامت به نقره‌های پخش‌وپلا در هوا گوش

می‌دهد.

از صدای انبوه رستوران‌های منتهی به شهر که می‌گذرند، دیگر نمی‌بینیم که انیس و پسر شوخ‌وشنگ و گرسنه لمیده‌اند در تاکسی و چشم‌هاشان پیِ غذا می‌گردد. با این که نمی‌بینیم اما صدای جنگلی را می‌شنویم که شکارچیانش پیِ طعمه‌اند و همه جا را بو می‌کشند. دهانِ انیس یخچالِ قدیمیِ پسر را می‌خواهد، می‌خواهد بغلش کند و بعد ببوسدش تا یخچال اغوا شود و انبانِ غذایش را باز کند. ابروهای پسر طعمه‌یی را برِ خیابانی پیدا می‌کند. صدای ترمزِ تاکسی هوار می‌شود بر بوقِ ماشین‌های دیگر.

۱۰

صدای بوقِ تلفن روی اعصابِ انیس که راه برود،
منشیِ انتشارات با بازدمی برخورنده گوشی را برمی‌دارد؛
داشته ناخن‌ها را سوهان می کشیده و وقفه‌یی بین‌شان
افتاده شاید. صدای انیس لب‌ولوچه‌اش را جمع می کند و با
لبخند از منشی می‌خواهد که وصل کند به مدیرِ انتشارات.
منشی نگاهی می‌اندازد به انگشتِ اشاره‌ی دستِ راستش که
نیمه‌سوهان‌خورده لولیده در سیمِ تلفن. صدای انیس خودش
را جمع‌وجورتر می کند تا لبخندش از پشتِ گوشی در چشمِ
مدیر بهتر دیده شود.

صدای مدیر متعجب می‌شود از این که مزدرانی
چه‌طور تا این لحظه به انیس کارِ ویرایش نداده. صدای انیس
هم رنگِ تعجب می گیرد از این بی‌اطلاعیِ مدیر. در این‌جا

بهتر است تقبی بزنیم به ذهنِ انیس، چون احتمال می‌دهد مدیر خبر داشته باشد و به رویِ خودش نمی‌آورد یا اصلاً دستورِ خودش بوده به مزدرانی که دیگر به او کار ندهد و دست‌به‌سرش کند. بعد دوباره برمی‌گردیم به صدای انیس پشتِ گوشی که حالا دیگر رنگ باخته و صدای مدیر که می‌گوید به مزدرانی خبر می‌دهم همین الان تماس بگیرد و یك کار برایت پیش از رفتن به شیراز کنار بگذارد.

دستِ انیس به‌اتفاقِ گوشی در فضای کوچكِ اتاقِ با تختیِ دو طبقه هم‌گامِ پاها راه می‌رود. صدای باز و بسته شدنِ پلك‌های انیس. کندیِ صداها، نفس‌ها. مکث‌های هرازگاه و سر چرخاندن‌ها. در یکی از آن پلك‌زدن‌ها ناگاه چشمِ انیس می‌افتد به کوله‌پشتی. به‌سمتش می‌رود که گوشیِ انیس زنگ می‌خورد و صدای مزدرانی چشم می‌درانَد و نعره می‌زند که فعلاً کاری برای ویرایش نداریم و هر وقت داشتیم خبرت می‌کنیم. صدای پلكِ انیس که بسته می‌شود.

۱۱

صدای سردردِ انیس در صبحِ خیابان وقتی دستش از دستِ پسر جدا می‌شود. صدای ازدحامِ پیاده‌رو و دستِ انیس که گوشی‌اش را از جیبش درمی‌آورد تا اس‌ام‌اسی بخواند. صدای کُندشدن و بعد ایستادنِ انیس در پیاده‌رو. صدای نگاهِ انیس بر اطرافِ پیاده‌رو.

انیس شبِ آخر برای پسر از اس‌ام‌اسِ عماد می‌گوید که وقتی آن روز صبح از پسر جدا شده به او زده. عماد ظاهراً سایشِ شانه‌های انیس و پسر را در آن سرعتِ تاکسیِ زرد یا سبزی که سوارش بوده دیده و رنگِ لب‌ها و چشم‌هاشان را در آن صبحِ خیابان لمس کرده. طاقتش نَم کشیده و بعد از ماه‌ها اس‌ام‌اس زده به انیس و هر چه بد و بیراه بوده هوار کرده سرِ پسر. انیس جواب نداده، اما عماد چند ساعت بعدتر که با

رفیقش، مزدرانی، تلفنی حرف زده، انگار کشف کرده پسر کیست و باز اس‌ام‌اس داده به انیس. انیس چشم‌هاش را بسته، پاهاش را درازبه‌دراز روی تخت سُرانده و باز جمع کرده و در ذهن گذرانده چه لحظه‌های خوبی با عماد داشته، اما لبِ انیس خشک شده بوده و لبخندش ماسیده. دستِ انیس بی‌هوا گوشی را برداشته و زنگ زده به مزدرانی. صدای مزدرانی لرزیده وقتی در جوابِ انیس هول کرده و گفته اول او به عماد زنگ زده، و بعد دستِ انیس عصبانی گوشی را قطع کرده. صدای خش‌خش و تخلخل در سردردِ انیس.

کوله‌پشتیِ انیس سریده می‌شود روی تخت تا می‌رسد زیرِ چانه و بعدتر نگاهِ انیس. صدای سریده‌شدن شاید خیلی به ترسیمِ فضا کمکی نکند، اما حواس‌مان باشد که باز و بسته‌شدنِ پلک‌های انیس مهم است، به‌خصوص بسته‌شدنِ پلک‌ها...
ندیدن‌های انیس. هم‌زمان با نگاهِ انیس، فضای کوچکِ اتاق را می‌بینیم و یك تختِ دو طبقه با انیس و کوله‌پشتی، که حالا دیگر زیپش باز شده و دستِ انیس که انگار کورمالی مدام است. چیزی از درونِ کوله‌پشتی بیرون نمی‌آید اصلاً، چشم‌های انیس بسته‌تر می‌شود، پلك‌ها کم‌تر، کُندتر. شب.

۱۳

می‌شنویم که دستِ انیس و شراب می‌رقصند در جوارِ کتابخانه‌ی پسر. صدای شبِ آخر. صدای پسر که نشسته کنارِ انیس و میزِ هشت گوش. صدای موهای انیس وقتی سَر می گرداند تا در چشم‌های پسر برق بزند. صدای چك‌چكِ آب و یخچال. صدای لب‌ها و گونه‌ها. صدای چشم‌ها.

صدای شانه‌های انیس که در چشم‌های پسر و شراب قهقاه می گیرد هراز گاه. صدای جام‌ها، پشتِ هم سرِ هم. صدای شب. شبِ آخر.

صدای پلك‌هایِ برابرِ هم. صدای زمان. صدای جامِ آخر و شکلات. صدای تنِ انیس و پسر وقتی به اتفاق می‌افتند روی تخت. صدای مدامِ شب. صدای مزه‌مزه کردنِ لب‌ها. صدای نوری که می‌دود در رگ‌ها. صدای نفس‌ها و گرمیِ

شرابی که در دهان‌شان دست‌به‌دست می‌شود. صدای تن.
صدای شبِ آخر.

زمان با پله‌های اتوبوسِ مسافری پایان می‌گیرد که کفش‌های انیس بی‌هوا روی‌شان به اصطکاک در می‌آید. باید حواس‌مان جمع باشد که فاصله‌ی زمانی برخوردِ کفش‌ها را با هر پله درست شرح دهیم. در هر اصطکاک صداهای اطرافِ اتوبوس پررنگ‌تر می‌شود و سرعت دارد، اما صدای خودِ اصطکاک کند و بم است؛ گوش را نمی‌خراشد. اما در این‌جا می‌مانیم. صداهای اطراف زیاد است و دقیق می‌شویم به گفت‌وگوهای کوتاهِ مسافران و خدمه‌ی اتوبوس؛ بیش‌ترِ حرف‌ها حولِ مقصدِ اتوبوس و زمانِ حرکت و بارهای مسافران می‌گردد. از پله‌ی آخری که کفش‌های انیس روی‌اش چرخی می‌خورد تا به صندلی‌اش برسد تا آن‌جا که دست‌های انیس کوله‌پشتی‌اش را درمی‌آورد تا در بالای سرش جاسازی

کند، هیچ نمی‌بینیم؛ حتا چشم‌هاش را که وقتِ گذر از راه‌باریکه‌ی بینِ صندلی‌ها دوان و چرخان به دیگران می‌افتد. ما آرامشِ تنش را می‌بینیم که لم داده بر صندلی. ثبتِ نورِ داخلِ اتوبوس در این‌جا اهمیتِ بسیار دارد. صداها هم، کم‌تر البته. بعد همه چیز در سفیدی فرو می‌رود.

ضمیمه

(باز هم شب)

انتشارات

صدای پک‌هایی که پسر به سیگار می‌زند صبح در
بالکنِ انتشارات.
صدای کتری که در سرش می کوبد. صدای چای.
صدای شکسته‌شدنِ لیوانی که وقتِ ظرف‌شستن
رسوخ می کند در فضای انتشارات.
صدای پیراهنِ منصور خان وقتی با منشی آمرانه
صحبت می کند به مددِ حرکتِ دست‌ها.
صدای جیرجیرِ درِ ورودیِ انتشارات؛ صدای لبخندِ
مدیر در فضای اتاق‌ها.
صدای شوخِ چشم‌های پسر وقتی با انیس حرف می‌زند
در تلفن.

صدای اهلِ قلم در اتاقِ انتظار.

صدای عاصیِ سیمِ تلفنِ منشی که رنگِ استراحت به خود نمی‌بیند.

صدای پر و پخشِ افسانه در اتاق‌های مختلف. صدای قدم‌های سریعش. صدای درها که باز و بسته می‌شود مدام و صدای زبانِ افسانه که قرار ندارد بین‌شان.

صدای گوش‌های مزدرانی که تیز می‌شود برای هر چیز.

صدای سانسور. صدای قهقهه. صدای خشم. صدای نگرانیِ مدیر از مثله‌شدن کتاب‌ها.

صدای انگشتِ شستِ پسر که بر روی دکمه‌های موبایل می‌لغزد.

صدای ناهار وقتی آشپزخانه در ازدحامِ آدم‌ها نفس می‌کشد.

صدای انیس وقتی پسر چشم‌هاش را می‌بندد. صدای انیس. صدای انیس.

افسانه

۱. یك روز صبح افسانه از خواب بیدار می‌شود و در آینه‌ی دستشویی که خودش را برانداز می کند، یادِ آن عصری می‌افتد که مزدرانی به بهانه‌ی تبریكِ عید لب بر گونه‌های او و باقیِ دخترانِ انتشارات گذاشته بود... و یکهو بالا می آورد.

۲. افسانه تنها زند گی می کند و مستأجر است. صبحانه را به‌همراهیِ آهنگ‌های کلاسیك می‌خورد.

۳. آب‌وتاب که در صدای مزدرانی افتاد، صدای پلك پریدن‌هاش قرار گرفت. دکتر گفته بود مشکلِ اعصاب دارد و باید مراعات کند. افسانه صداش را نرم کرد اما حرفی نزد. آب‌وتابِ صدا شق‌ورق ایستاده بود و پایین

نمی آمد؛ در انتظارِ حرفی، آمدنِ لغتی از دهانِ دیگری بود. ابروهای افسانه مهربان شد و دلسوزی کرد.

۴. «دروغ می گوید مزدرانی، اما می گفت به‌ش زنگ زده‌اند و با خنده گفته‌اند که دو شبِ دیگر می آییم دنبالت دمِ خانه. با نیشخند حالی‌اش کرده بودند که بهتر است خانه را از اسناد و هر چیزِ دیگر پاك کند. می گفت شبِ موعد خواب از چشمش رفته بوده و تا پنج‌ونیمِ صبح که زنگ خانه را بزنند، در تختش همین‌طور غلتیده و صدای فنرهای تخت را در گوشِ فهیمه و بچه‌ی کوچك‌شان به آواز درآورده. فهیمه مانتو و روسری‌اش را از عصر تنش کرده بوده که اگر ریختند داخلِ خانه، آماده باشد.

«داخل که نیامده بودند هیچ، ازش محترمانه خواسته بودند بیاید پایین. سوارِ ماشینش کرده بودند و مجبورش کرده بودند تا وقتی نگفته‌اند چشم‌هاش را ببندد. می گفت در راه از صداشان فهمیده که سه نفرند. جرأت نکرده بود چشم‌هاش را باز کند.

«داخلِ ساختمانی می‌شوند و از آسانسور همراه با آن سه صدا بالا می‌روند و بعد آن یکی که زیر بغلش را گرفته می‌بردش داخلِ اتاقی و مجبورش می کند بی که چشم باز

کند بنشیند روی صندلی. می گفت اول صدای هرمِ نفس‌های یکی از آن سه نفر را زیرِ لاله‌ی گوشش حس می کند و بعد یکهو فریاد مرد پرده‌ی گوشش را به سوت می کشد. بعد کنارِ آن یکی گوشش صدای نفسِ یکی دیگر هم اضافه می‌شود. می گفت لاله‌ی گوشِ اولی هنوز در گیجیِ صدای فریاد خشکش زده بود.

«بالاخره صدای یکی از آن سه نفر درمی‌آید و بهش می‌فهماند که کارهاش اقدام علیه امنیت ملی است. اما کدام کار؟

«خلاصه، می گفت بعد از چند ساعت داد و بیداد و تهدید، دوباره سوارِ ماشینش کرده بودند و بعد در همان حوالیِ انتشارات ازش خواسته بودند که از ماشین پیاده شود و تا پنجاه بشمارد و بعد چشم‌هاش را باز کند.»

۵. افسانه به عرقِ تن و بوی آدم‌ها حساس است. چندشش می‌شود. تابستان که می‌شود عزا می گیرد که چه‌طور مزدرانی را تحمل کند، اما به آنی دلش می‌سوزد براش.

۶. یک‌بار در آن شلوغی‌های بعد از انتخابات آن‌قدر کتک خورد که تنش کبود شد افسانه. از آن به بعد بی‌خوابی امانش را گرفت.

منصور خان

۱. وقتِ ناهار مزدرانی و منصور خان در آشپزخانه‌ی انتشارات تنها چیزی که می‌خورند سالاد است. هر دو استخوان‌بندیِ درشتی دارند و چاق‌اند، با این تفاوت که منصور خان دست‌های کوتاهی دارد و تقریباً بی گردن است. برای همین، همیشه پیراهنی می‌پوشد که یقه‌یی پهن دارد. صدای چنگالش که به تهِ ظرفِ سالاد برسد، می‌شنوی که از کمر به بالا سنگینیِ سایه‌اش افتاده روی ظرف.

۲. منصور خان بعد از آن‌که یك کارخانه‌ی مدادسازی را تحتِ مدیریتِ خود به ورشکستگی کشاند و پول‌هایش را با زرنگیِ خاصی بالا کشید، پیشِ شریكِ قدیمی‌اش در انتشارات بازگشت و شد مدیرِ مالی و فروشِ

انتشارات.

۳. منصور خان همیشه وسواسش را در صدای شیرِ آب و دست‌شستن خلاصه می‌کند.

۴. «من خیلی به چلغوزِ کفتر معتقدم. یک‌بار قرار بود قراردادی ببندم با شرکتی برای صادرات. دو دل بودم. پیاده راه افتادم به‌سمتِ محلِ قرار. در راه، جلوی پایم ناگهان چلغوزی از آسمان افتاد. تردید نکردم. قرار را لغو کردم و برگشتم خانه. بعدها اعضای هیئت‌مدیره متوجه شدند که چه‌قدر من درست عمل کرده‌ام.»

۵. صبح به صبح مزدرانی بو می‌کشد تا ببیند کی عطرِ منصور خان در فضای انتشارات منتشر است. عصر به عصر، وقتِ رفتن، صدای دستِ خداحافظی‌شان راه‌پله‌ی ساختمانِ انتشارات را مرتعش می‌کند.

۶. منصور خان پس از سرکوبیِ شلوغی‌های بعد از انتخابات، وقتی با مزدرانی از پله‌های ساختمانِ انتشارات پایین می‌آمدند، سکته‌ی ناقص کرد. از آن به بعد بی‌خوابی امانش را گرفت و خانه‌نشین شد.

دری که ورق می خورد